Made To Be You

Written by: Bob Genisot

Illustrated by: Maggie Joy

Made To Be You

Written by Bob Genisot

Illustrated by Maggie Joy

Edited by Marla McKenna

Layout by Michael Nicloy

Paperback ISBN 978-1-957351-41-4

Published by
Nico 11 Publishing & Design
Mukwonago, Wisconsin
www.nico11publishing.com

Quantity orders may be placed with the publisher via email:
mike@nico11publishing.com
Printed in The United States of America

You made all the delicate, inner parts of my body
and knit me together in my mother's womb.
Thank you for making me so wonderfully complex!
Your workmanship is marvelous—how well I know it.

– Psalm 139:13–14 (NLT)

Once upon a time there was a lump of clay.
The lump of clay was sitting on a
shelf in the studio of a Potter.

Now, this Potter was a master sculptor
and famous throughout the area.

One day the Potter got the lump of clay down and took it to
the sculpting table. The Potter started to mold it and work
it with incredible skill and precision. He spun the clay,
forming it with perfection.
The lump of clay, which was now taking on the shape
of a small pot, was then fired in the kiln, making it firm and
durable. When the clay cooled, the Potter took it out and
painted it with great detail and precision. The potter then
glazed it, fired it again, did some touch-up work, and made
small corrections until the pot was finally done.

The Potter looked at the finished pot and smiled. It was put on a sturdy wooden shelf next to other master works. They were all gorgeous. In fact, the potter's projects ran the gamut of all different sizes, shapes, and virtually every color you could imagine.

Beaming with excitement, the pot thought to itself,
"I wonder what great thing I was made to be?"

Sometime later a young couple came into the Potter's studio. The couple was very much in love, joyfully laughing and talking as they admired the Potter's work. After carefully inspecting several beautiful pieces, they stopped abruptly at the pot. They were completely drawn to it. They both seemed excited as they picked the pot up and turned it over repeatedly with discussion. Finally, they put the pot on the counter, purchased it, and headed out.
The pot thought to itself, "Now I finally get to find out what I was made to be!"

All Plants on Sale!

"Take this in remembrance."
the House

The couple brought the pot into their home, a modest two-
bedroom ranch on the outskirts of the city. Almost immediately,
the pot was filled with cool water from the tap, and a beautiful
bouquet of freshly cut flowers was unwrapped and placed neatly
into it.
The pot thought, "I must be something special! In fact, a beautiful
young couple like this must
think I'm very attractive to
hold such beautiful flowers!"

The couple's friends, who were
also nice-looking, incidentally,
seemed to think the pot
was pretty special, as well.
Because the couple's guests
always looked and pointed
whenever the pot got to show
off a vibrant display of flowers.
Sometimes it would be a small
arrangement of wildflowers,
and other times, on special
occasions, a dozen red roses. The couple was always smiling and
happy whenever they were around the pot, which was pleased with
what it was being used for.

However, one day the pot noticed a smell. And it wasn't a sweet, fragrant, flowery smell. The more recent display of flowers was withered and the water was stagnant. The couple must have noticed it, too, as they hurriedly dumped the flowers out and rinsed out the pot. But no one replaced the flowers as they did before. In fact, many months went by. The pot was cleaned and dried and stored in a small cabinet above the sink.

Be Still And Know.
S P
Bread Flour
Whole Wheat
Rolled Oats
Brown Sugar
White Sugar

The pot thought to itself, "Well, maybe I'm not so attractive after all. I guess that's why I'm not needed anymore."

A short time later, the wife reached for the pot in the cabinet and placed it into a small cardboard box. The box was brought outside on a table with a bunch of other things: a newer toaster, a lamp, some old clothes. The pot was unboxed and neatly placed on the table next to the other items. Soon, the driveway was filled with people rummaging through the items on the tables.

There were kids laughing and playing tag while nimbly avoiding the tables full of fragile items. The pot suddenly felt a bump, and tumbled onto the grass. One of the kids grabbed the pot and started to toss it around. The pot was scared at first but then felt a new kind of energy and excitement. The pot was soon whisked away by a parent of one of the kids and bagged with other items in the dark trunk of their car.

When the family got out, the kids reached into the trunk, grabbed the pot, and started swinging it. Again, nervous, but intrigued, the pot thought, "Hey, this is fun! I've never had fun like this before!"

And, the fun didn't stop! In fact, whenever the kids were around, the pot was always used for something fun, like tossing ping-pong balls inside, using the pot as a step stool to reach a high shelf (that kind of hurt), enlisting the pot to be some sort of helmet for an action figure, and countless other fun activities.

The pot thought to itself, "I must be made to have fun and entertain people! I love this!"

But all of a sudden, that fun and entertainment stopped. The kids seemed too busy. Oh sure, every once in a while, one of them would turn the pot upside down and drum it with a pencil, but it just wasn't the same.

The pot found itself wedged between a stuffed animal and plastic tote in the back of a closet, laying on its side, and thinking to itself, "Well, maybe I'm not so fun to be around after all. I guess that's why I'm not needed anymore."

A few months later, the closet door opened, and the pot was extracted out from the midst of a few tons of clothes. The pot found itself back in a vehicle--a nice one--that stopped near a tall building in a city. The driver got out and grabbed a briefcase and the pot.

The driver entered the building, walked down a beautifully tiled hallway that stopped at an elevator. Entering with a small group of similarly-destined people, they ascended to the top floor. The space that awaited the pot was an office with large windows. The view was amazing! This time, instead of a kitchen table, the pot sat on a desk next to a bunch of family pictures, a phone, and a computer. People wearing suits and carrying folders walked in and out of the office constantly. The pot felt a weird jab at its base. It was something sharp the pot later learned that was used to open letters. Soon the pot became filled with other items, such as pencils, pens, and markers, which were constantly being taken in and out.

The pot soon realized, "This is a really important person and I'm helping this person do a lot of really important things! I must have been made to work! This feels amazing!"

The pot felt so important! It didn't mind the late evenings, the early mornings, the constant jabs from pencils and pens thrown in, and that sharp letter opener! The pot was also a source for highlighters, a pocket knife, some keys, and even the occasional pack of gum or mints. In fact, the pot was so versatile, when those huge windows were vented, it was even used to hold down important papers in the wind!

For years, the office space was a hub of activity. The pot relished its quiet time on the weekends, when only the cleaning crew was present. But then one weekend seemed unusually long. Abnormally long. Longer than a typical vacation. The building was dark with no activity. Not even vacuuming. The pot lost count after 15 sunrises.
What happened?
The pot thought to itself, "Wow. Maybe I'm not a good worker anymore. I guess that's why I'm not needed."

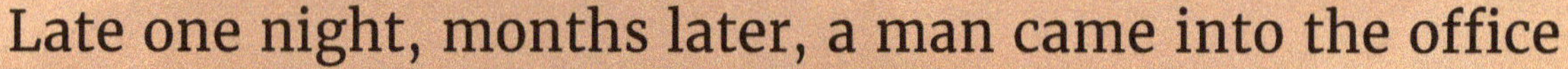

Late one night, months later, a man came into the office
space and loaded a bunch of items
into a box, including the pot.
After the short ride on the elevator
down to the lower level, the man took
the box outside, setting it by the front
door. He repeated this pattern several more
times over the next few hours--boxes stacked
three and four high.
An old pickup truck stopped early the next morning
and a small crew took the boxes, all of them, and
loaded them into the bed. It was a noisy, bumpy
trip. The truck arrived at a building, though not
like the big office.
This one was smaller and had few windows
and no view. The lights came on, and the pot
noticed the building was
filled with shelves
containing all sorts
of things.

After the pot was roughly lifted out of the box and put onto a
glass shelf, it could get a better view of the items in this store.
There were old record albums, picture frames, a ripped painting,
broken vase, and a number of chipped plates.
"Here's one. Welcome to your new home," the pot overheard
from nearby. It was an orange gravy boat. "Thanks. Hi," the pot
retorted back.

The glass display the pot was placed on had an old scratched mirror. For the first time in its life, the pot saw itself. It took a good, long look at itself and knew--it knew it didn't belong. It wasn't like the other items. They were rough, broken, and defective. The pot didn't want to be there.

But the more time that went on, the pot decided this place wasn't so bad. The other items were welcoming and accepting. They all had similar experiences. They were all given away, or sold, tossed out, left behind, abandoned, and otherwise forgotten about. Just like the pot was several times before now. The pot realized that it had finally found others that understood. The pot thought to itself, "I may not be beautiful, or fun, or a hard worker, but at least I have friends now." In fact, the pot, who used to hate it when it got dirty or smelly, now welcomed the dust and grime because it was a way to fit in with the rest of the items in the store.

Yes, the misfit knickknacks and housewares did indeed have a good time, but every night before the store owner closed and turned the lights off, the pot would look at itself in the mirror and think, "I don't belong here, but I just don't belong anywhere else." And, the pot would be very sad.

Knives
Hunting Rifles
GUNS
OPEN
PAWN
SHOP
BUY-SELL-TRADE
25¢ each
All items in glass case on sale
Keep hands off glass.
Ring bell for assistance
Records
VHS
Vinyl Players

So, this was the case for many years. Until one early
afternoon, the pot heard the familiar jingle from
the front door bell. All of the items, including
the pot, would have a glimmer of excitement
at the prospect of being rescued from this
place of despair (though they never talked
about it). The pot overheard the customer
talking to the store owner. It was strange.
That voice sounded familiar. Was it a friend of
that young couple? A coworker in the big office building?
No, but it was definitely a voice the pot had heard before.
The voice was getting louder and clearer. Before the pot
could make another guess, it was forcefully lifted off the shelf.

The pot hadn't been off the shelf
in years, and it was feeling very
embarrassed and self-conscious
due to the filthy condition it was
in. The customer scraped the
palm of their hand across the pot's
surface to wipe off the thick layer of
built-up dust. Astonished, the pot
finally recognized the customer--
it was the Potter!

The Potter smiled. The pot hadn't seen a smile
in years. It was reminiscent of the smiles the
pot used to get from the young couple, and
from the kids when they were playing, but
it was altogether different. No, the Potter's
smile was the very same smile the pot saw
when it was first created.

Too fixated on that smile that
brought such indescribable
joy, the pot almost missed
the words the Potter said,
over and over, as they
headed towards the door,
"My masterpiece!
My masterpiece is back!"

The pot could scarcely recall the trip back to the Potter's studio. But when they arrived, the pot could easily remember the sounds, the sights, the smells. In the weeks and months to follow, the pot was used to hold paint and glazing brushes, scrapers--one time it even held candy (this naturally brought people joy).

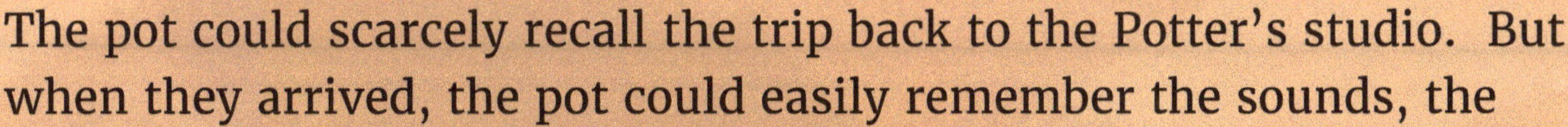

Sometimes the pot was on display to attract customers who entered the studio. Whatever the Potter needed, the pot was eager to help. "I finally know what great thing I was made to be- ME!" the pot proudly realized. The pot, perhaps for the first time, was truly happy and peaceful.

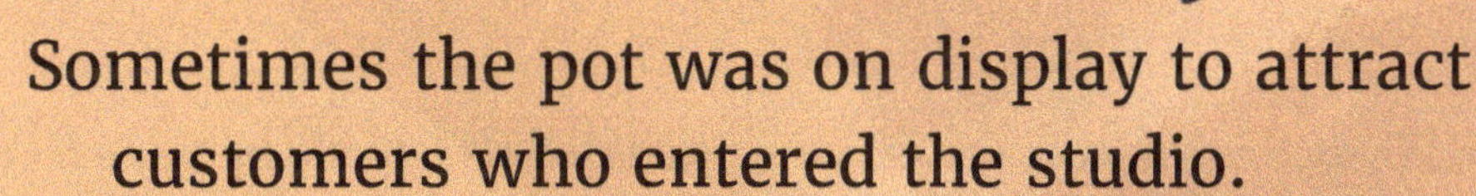

Then one day the Potter took the pot, and removed the small handful of brushes that it contained, and carefully rinsed the residue out from the bottom. "This has happened before," the pot thought to itself, "I must be getting prepared for a new assignment."
The cleaned pot was subsequently filled with warm water and deliberately placed in a portion of the studio that seemed completely foreign to the pot. The pot saw the Potter reach up and grab something off of a shelf and place it next to the pot. Clay. A lump of clay. Suddenly, the pot heard a familiar sound--one that it had heard strongly just once before--when it was first formed. The pot got its first ever view of the very same process that it went through countless years prior. The molding, the shaping, the cutting, the correcting. The pot saw the master craftsmanship of the Potter first-hand. As the brand new, unsuspecting lump started to take form, the Potter would frequently dip his hands into the warm water held by the pot.
As the process continued, the pot thought to itself, "I've never felt more useful in my entire life!"

The wheel stopped and the Potter removed the new project. The
pot knew what came next--the firing, the glazing, the painting,
more firing, the touch-up work, and the final corrections.
The pot could hardly contain itself wondering what this new
masterpiece--one that the pot helped to create--would look like?

The Potter looked at the new finished product and smiled. THAT
smile. That very same smile that the pot so vividly remembered
and could recall at any time.

No one--not the couple, or the kids, or even the gravy boat--made the pot feel more special or more loved than the Potter did, with just that smile! This new project was placed gently down in front of the pot. It looked very different--different size, shape, color, it was more of a bowl, really--but it was oddly similar to the pot.
The last thing the Potter did to complete his new masterpiece was to stamp his initials--his insignia--on the bottom of the bowl in such a manner that it couldn't ever be removed. Anyone who would ever encounter that bowl from this point forward would know beyond a shadow of a doubt who created it.
The pot still remembered when it was stamped by the Potter. It was something the pot was always proud of, even during its darkest and most uncertain times.

Placed back upright, the bowl now sat directly
next to the pot. It was gorgeous. In fact, it was
about the most perfect thing the pot had even seen.
Beaming with excitement, the pot thought to itself,
"I wonder what great thing it was made to be?"

About the Author

Bob Genisot loved children's books as a kid, and probably loves them even more as an adult. The countless hours he spent reading to his two boys before bedtime are some of his most cherished memories. His writing style and substance reflect both the simple joys of youth and the precious promises of God. Bob and his wife, Sandra, lead Brilliance Ministries and are passionate about encouraging others to use their gifts, talents, and abilities for the Glory of God.

About the Illustrator

Maggie Joy Tanner is a local Alaskan artist who has been pursuing many creative avenues all her life. She first fell in love with the arts as a little girl watching her mother (a highly experienced artist) make watercolor painting look effortless. Maggie has since been inspired to venture into the world of illustrations and digital arts. With the support of her wonderful family and loving community, she has learned that to create something out of nothing aligns us with our Creator in a very unique and personal way. Maggie's desire is that God's own fingerprint shows up in every little piece she stewards.

www.ingramcontent.com/pod-product-compliance
Lightning Source LLC
Chambersburg PA
CBHW042107160726
48295CB00017B/1018